Copyright © 2017 by Laura Jaworski

Illustration Copyright © 2017 by Laura Jaworski

All rights reserved. No part of this publication may be reproduced, distributed, or transmitted in any form or by any means, including photocopying, recording, or other electronic or mechanical methods, without the prior written permission of the author and illustrator.

Printed in the United States of America

First Printing, 2017

ISBN 978-1547259861

www.laurajaworski.com

To Pat, who believes so dearly in the goodness of helping others. ♡

Mr. Gnome's Home

by Laura Jaworski

In a charming little forest
With a touch of silver-gold
Lies a quiet scene just waiting
For a story to unfold…

Let's watch, shall we?

Pitter-patter, do you hear that?
Here comes someone marching home
With a cap and grumbling tummy
Ah! It must be Mr. Gnome.

Here he comes now through the forest
With a satchel on his back
Sleepy eyes and great big yawn
I'll bet he's ready for a nap!

Up the steps into his treehouse
What a cozy little home
Roaring fire, tea and crumpets
Simply perfect for a gnome!

Now beside the crickle-crackle
In a bed of softest down
Little eyes begin to slide shut—
Hang a minute, what's that sound?

Tap-tap-tap upon the window
Knock-knock-knock upon the door
Rumble-bumble, goodness me!
It's even shaking up the floor!

Why, a little woodland fairy!
And a friend, plus hundreds more!
What a jam, they all exclaim
You see, there's going to be a storm!

Do come in! Yes you, and you there
Squeeze right past, we'll find the room
WHOOSH—the wind!
And SPLASH—the raindrops!
Seems the storm will be here soon!

Safe inside while thunder rumbles
Mr. Gnome runs back and forth
For it's helping those in need, he says
That gives his home its mirth.

All night long they crowd together
Sipping tea and snuggling 'round
With the whistling winds and rainfall
Muffled out by other sounds…

Why, there's jesting and there's laughter
And there's storytelling, too
I couldn't plan a better party
For a finer crowd, could you?

Here comes dawn, it's softly breaking
And the sun will be up soon
Wave hello to morning dewdrops
Send farewells up to the moon.

The storm has passed, it's time for breakfast
Stack the kindling, slice the bread
Hang about, where's Mr. Gnome?
Why, he's fast asleep in bed!

Quiet down now, everybody
Let's surprise him when he wakes
Fairies, tidy
Elves can dust, and Dragon
You can bake the cake!

On he sleeps, and so it seems
Our story's coming to an end
But when he wakes our Mr. Gnome will find
One hundred brand-new friends!

The End!

For more books and fun visit
www.laurajaworski.com

Made in the USA
Lexington, KY
15 November 2017